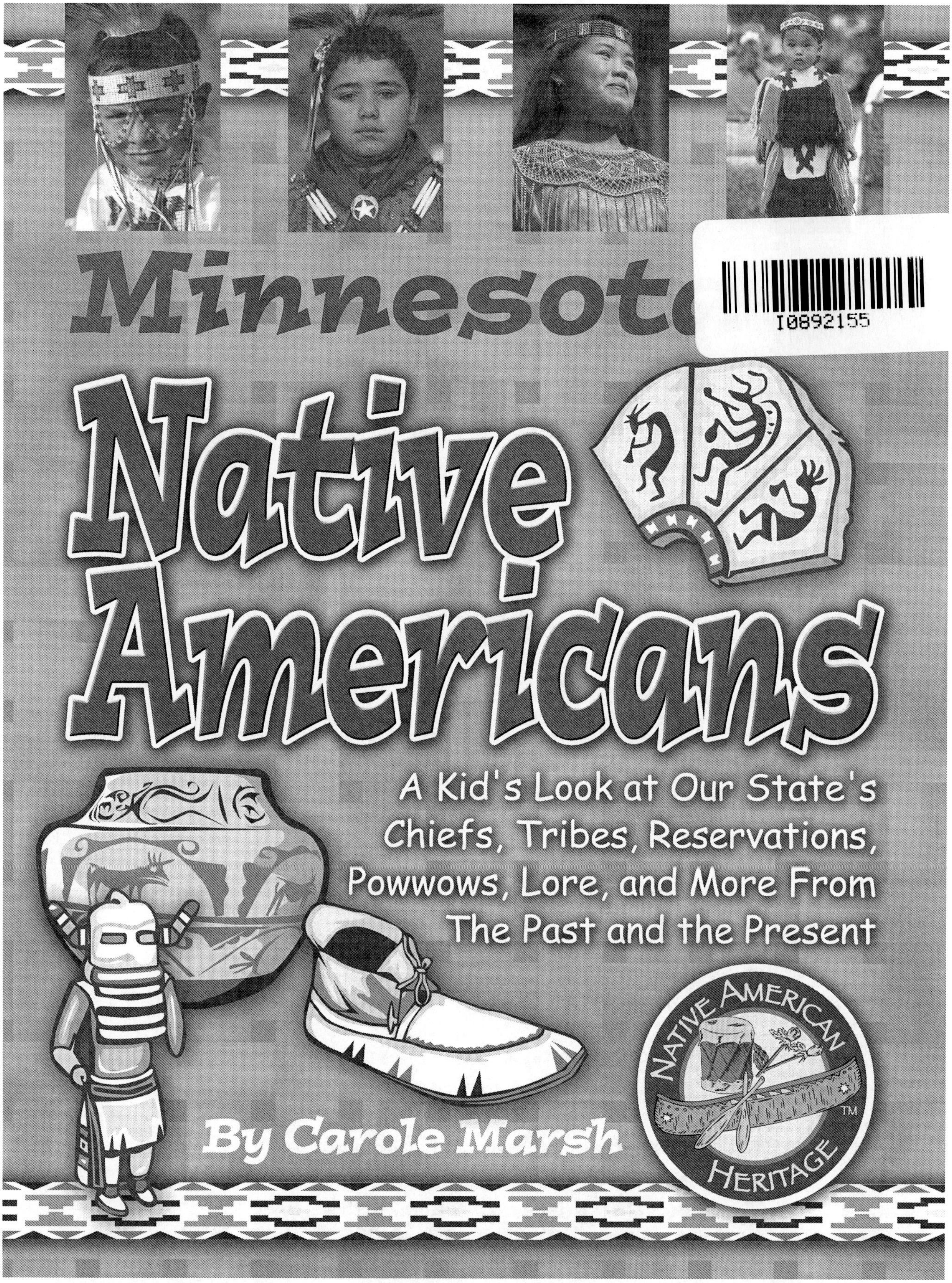

Graphic Design: Lynette Rowe • Cover Design: Victoria DeJoy

Published by
GALLOPADE™ INTERNATIONAL
800-536-2GET
www.gallopade.com

Gallopade is proud to be a member of these educational organizations and associations:

The National School Supply and Equipment Association (NSSEA)
American Booksellers Association (ABA)
Virginia Educational Media Association (VEMA)
Association of Partners for Public Lands (APPL)
Museum Store Association (MSA)
National Association for Gifted Children (NAGC)
Publishers Marketing Association (PMA)
International Reading Association (IRA)
Association of African American Museums (AAAM)

Native American Heritage™ Series

Native American Big Activity Book

Native American Biographies

Native American Coloring Book

Native American Heritage Book

Native American Timeline

Minnesota State Stuff™

- My First Pocket Guide: Minnesota
- My First Book About Minnesota
- Minnesota Coloring Book
- The Big Minnesota Reproducible Activity Book
- Jeopardy: Answers & Questions About Our State
- Minnesota "Jography!": A Fun Run Through Our State
- Minnesota Gamebooks
- Minnesota Bingo Games
- Minnesota Illustrated Timelines
- Minnesota Project Books
- Minnesota Bulletin Board Set
- Minnesota PosterMap
- Minnesota Stickers
- Let's Discover Minnesota! CD-ROM

Word from the Author

Hello!

I hope you are as interested in North America's wonderful Indian heritage as I am!

Like most kids, I grew up thinking of Indians as the other half of Cowboys. Today, of course, we are getting a much clearer and more accurate picture of what the first peoples on our land were all about. These "facts" are much more fascinating than anything Hollywood can make up. And you probably won't find much of this information in your history textbook!

I am 1/16 Cherokee. This is something I am very proud of and happy about. My grandmother was 1/4 Cherokee. She had tan skin, long gray hair and a very Indian look – especially if I did something bad! Her maiden name was Carrie Corn. Of course, when she got married, she took her husband's name, so it was many years before I learned to appreciate the significance of my native heritage.

Today, I'm trying to make up for lost time by exploring my roots as deeply as I can. One of the most interesting things I've learned is how fascinating all of the Indian tribes are – in the past, the present and future!

As you read about "your" Indians, remember that all native peoples were part of an ever-changing network of time, ideas, power and luck — good and bad. This is certainly a history that is not "dead," but continues to change – often right outside our own back doors! – all the time.

Carole Marsh
She-Who-Writes

PS: Many references show different spellings for the same word. I have tried to select the most common spelling for the time period described. I would not want to be in an Indian spelling bee!

A is for . . .

Arrowhead Country

A region in Minnesota's Superior Upland in the northeast part of the state. Guess what you can find here?

Awl

An Indian's "needle." Often made from wood, thorns, bone, or metal, it was used to punch holes in skins so they could be sewn together.

Adze

An Indian woodworking tool used to cut, scrape, or gouge; often used to hollow dugout canoes. Blades were made of stone, shell, bone or copper.

Assiniboine

This tribe's name in the Chippewa language means "those who cook with stones", referring to stone-boiling. Early in their history, they were one people with the Sioux and lived in northern Minnesota. They later split from the Sioux and migrated west to the northern plains of the U.S. and Canada.

Agriculture

Early Minnesota Indians slowly learned to farm. Corn or maize was a staple crop. They used tools like stone axes to clear trees and bowls to grind corn.

Altar

A platform made of rocks or animal skulls; some had bowls, feathers, rattles, or skins on them. Indians prayed at these altars for things like good crops or expert hunting skills.

Arrow

A long, slender shaft made of reed, cane, or wood; pointed tip was attached to one end and split feathers to the other. Feathers helped the arrows fly straight.

Arrowhead

The pointed tip of an arrow, made of bone, antler, wood, or iron. Some tips had barbs that would embed themselves in flesh. These barbs made it difficult for an enemy to remove the arrowhead from a wound.

Aborigine

A member of the earliest known population of a region.

Arapaho

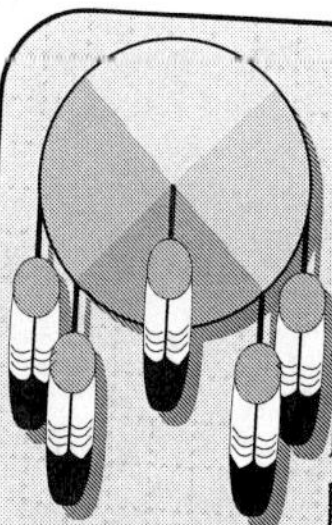

Famous Plains Indian raiding tribe that is believed to have originally lived in the Red River region of northern Minnesota. They migrated several times, with the tribe splitting twice along the way. They didn't adopt the Plains Indian ways until the 1800s, and became known as master horse trainers.

B is for . . .

Bullroarer

Sacred instrument symbolizing rain, lightning and thunder. Made of a rectangular piece of wood and a cord.

Band

A subdivision of an Indian tribe. In earlier times, a band was sometimes created when part of a tribe split off from the main group. The band also chose new leadership.

Blankets

Used for door covers, partitions, bags, to dry food on, carry babies and many other purposes.

Baskets

Some were woven and others were coiled. Baskets were made from roots, grasses, barks, and other natural materials.

Birch Coulee Park

Near Morton; site of an 1862 surprise attack by the Dakota Indians on Fort Ridgely soldiers who thought there were no more Indians in the region. The 30-hour battle resulted in the death of 20 soldiers.

Buckskin

Softened, smoke-treated rawhide. Used by Minnesota Indians to make clothes, bags and pouches.

Bow

Made from wood, horn or bone. Minnesota Indian children learned how to use bows. The bowstring was made from animal gut, rawhide or twisted vegetable fibers.

Bone

Animal bones were used by Minnesota Indians to make buttons, whistles and other items.

Beads

Made of wood, shells, claws, minerals, seeds — you name it! Later, the Minnesota Indians traded with white men for glass beads, used in some of their decorative arts.

C is for . . .

Cheyenne

Famous Plains Indian tribe that once lived in Minnesota, as late as the 1680s. While there, they lived in the woodland way. Migrated westward soon after that, living in the plains way after acquiring the horse.

Chief

Leader of a tribe. Different titles meant different things. Some members were made chief because they owned deeds to land. Chieftainship was often inherited, usually from the mother!

Contact Period

What historians call the era in the 1500s when Native Americans first met Europeans. This meeting changed the lifestyle of the Minnesota Indians more than anyone could ever have anticipated!

Calumet

Between 300 B.C. and A.D. 1000, Indians in the southwest corner of Minnesota mined a red stone called catlinite. From this stone they carved calumets, which were also called "peace pipes" or "war pipes." Refers to the stem of the pipe, which is decorated with feathers or carved to signal the tribe's intentions. Believed to have great power. The pipestone quarries became sacred ground; Indians would travel long distances to get the stone.

Confederacy

A union of different groups of people. A confederacy in Indian culture was a group of tribes that agreed not to fight with each other. They agreed to live peacefully. Sometimes the tribes shared culture and language.

Canoe

The Chippewa Indians used the sleek and swift lightweight birch-bark canoe that was so perfect for Minnesota's lakes and rivers.

Clan

A tribal unit. Members are descended from the same ancestor.

Citizenship

The Indian Citizenship Act of 1924 states all Indians born in the United States are citizens of the United States, and citizens of the states they live in, even though they may live on a reservation. They can vote. They pay most local, state and federal taxes, including sales taxes.

Chippewa

One of the largest and most powerful tribes in North America. Their native name is Anishinabe. This tribe (especially in Canada) is also called Ojibway. They lived in the western Great Lakes, and used birch bark for containers and construction material. They fished, farmed, hunted, and gathered.

Crooked Lake

Along its shores are hundreds of fading rock paintings; one clearly shows a sturgeon caught in a net.

D is for . . .

Dance

There were Indian dances for every occasion: war, peace, hunting, rain, good harvests, etc. Drums, rattles, and flutes of bone or reed provided the music. Dancers often chanted or sang while performing. Steps were not easy to learn and required consistent practice.

Descendants

The first Minnesota Indians were descendants of primitive hunters who crossed the Bering Strait from Asia to what is now Alaska. At that time, glacial ice still covered most of North America. These people were the true discoverers of the "New World!"

Disease

Minnesota Indians had no immunity to the diseases that white explorers, colonists and settlers brought to their lands. These diseases included smallpox, measles, tuberculosis and others, which ravaged the tribes in great epidemics that killed many, and sometimes all, members of a tribe.

Dakota

When Europeans first came to explore North America, the Dakota (Sioux) people were the main inhabitants of Minnesota. They had lived in the upper Midwest's forests and grasslands for centuries. They hunted, fished and grew crops; some hunted buffalo.

Dyes

Made of lichens, berries, roots, bark, plants, and other natural materials by Indians in Minnesota. Different colors were used depending on what materials were available and what objects were to be dyed.

Dishes

Made from clay, bark, wood, stone, and other materials, depending on what was available and what food they would be used for.

Dennis Banks

In the 1960s, he founded the American Indian Movement (AIM) with George Mitchell and Clyde Bellecourt in Minneapolis. The AIM has been one of the most active of the Indian political groups.

Dreams

Important in the Indian tradition. It was believed that dreams were the "windows" to the soul. Many thought a person's hidden desires were expressed in dreams.

E is for . . .

Eagle

An animal used in many Indian ceremonies. Eagle feathers attached to war bonnets and shields communicated an Indian's rank in his tribe and what kinds of deeds he had done. Feathers also adorned rattles, pipes, baskets, and prayer sticks.

Early Artisans

Around 6,000 years ago, early people in the Great Lakes region of Minnesota found the mineral copper in its pure form along the shores of Lake Superior. They pounded it into tools and weapons, probably becoming the first people in the world to use copper!

Eastman, Dr. Charles Alexander

Santee Dakota doctor and author. His Indian name was Ohiyesa, "The Winner," and he attended Beloit College in Wisconsin after living wild until he was 15 years old. He went on to organize 42 Indian YMCAs. He was born in 1858 in Redwood Falls, Minnesota.

Earrings

Medicine men sometimes pierced male and female ears at special ceremonies. Earrings, which cost parents or relatives a significant amount, symbolized wealth and distinction. The more earrings that an Indian wore, the greater his honor. Some earrings measured 12 inches in length!

Environment

Preserving the environment is important to preserving Native American heritage. For thousands of years, Native American tribes lived completely off the land. Farming, mining, pollution have all had a part in changing native environments.

Effigy Mound Culture

People who built earthen figures of birds, animals or people. Some in Minnesota are in the shape of birds, buffaloes, bears or snakes.

English

In the 1800s, the U.S. government built boarding schools for Indian children throughout the nation. Children were forced to leave their homes and families to live at these schools. They were required to learn English and not speak their native languages.

Epidemics

Few Indians possessed immunity to the deadly diseases, like smallpox and measles, which European explorers and settlers brought to the New World. As a result, great population loss took place. Sometimes entire tribes became extinct. Epidemics sparked by Hernando De Soto's expedition are estimated to have killed 75% of the native population in the New World.

F is for . . .

Fort Ridgley

On the north bank of the Minnesota River. In August, 1862, during the Dakota uprising, settlers sought refuge here. The Indians attacked but were stopped by artillery; they returned a few days later, but were thwarted again.

Fetish

These small objects were thought to hold the spirit of an animal or a part of nature. A fetish could be an object found in nature, such as bone or wood, or it could be a carved object. The fetish was usually small enough to be carried in a small bag or on a cord. The making and use of a fetish was kept secret by its owner and only shared with the one who inherited it.

Fishers

Early Minnesota peoples hunted and gathered to keep from starving. Later, they learned to fish. When they finally learned to farm crops, they were more able to settle down into villages, instead of needing to forage all the time.

Fire Drill

A device used by Indians to make fires which consisted of a stick and a piece of wood with a tight hole in it. The stick was twirled rapidly in the hole, creating friction that would ignite shredded grass or wood powder placed nearby to start a fire.

Farmers

Many Minnesota Indians, ancient and modern, have farming ways! Even pre-contact Indians tilled and irrigated, raising many important crops. Corn, cotton, beans, squash, melons, sunflowers, gourds, pumpkins and tobacco are all native Indian crops!

Federal Recognition

The United States government's official acknowledgement of a group of Indians as a tribe that is eligible for government benefits, programs and funds.

Footwear

Minnesota Indians wore different footwear depending on their tribe and environment. Moccasins were made mostly of animal skin. Sandals were made of rawhide or plant material.

Fur Trade

Begun when the Europeans came eager to grow rich from the pelts of animals. Trading had a powerful impact on the Indian. To get the newcomers' goods, Indians worked as trappers for the French. A flintlock gun cost 12 beaver pelts. But the ultimate cost was much more expensive — the loss of the Indian's way of life. Many Indians abandoned their traditional farming for trapping and came to depend on the Europeans.

G is for . . .

Games

Adults played ball and other games of chance or skill. Indian children spun tops, fought pretend battles, did target-shooting, walked on stilts, played hide and seek, or competed to see who could hold their breath the longest!

Guns

The Chippewa were the first Indians in Minnesota to get guns from the whites. This helped them drive the Dakota to the west.

Grand Mound

One of the largest Indian mounds in Minnesota and the largest burial mound in the upper midwest. It is on the Rainy River near International Falls, and no longer open to the public. However, you can see mounds in St. Paul at the Indian Mounds Park.

Gens

Group of related members from different tribes.

Gathering

Native Americans gathered natural materials for food, fuel, baskets, clothing, and housing. American Indians tribes also hunted to meet basic needs. Even though some tribes planted crops, most did some kind of gathering.

Gorgets

Beautiful ornaments hung around the neck or from ears; their significance, if any, is unknown.

Gourds

Hollowed-out shell of a gourd plant's dried fruit which often grew into a specific shape. Indians raised many species of gourds. They were used for spoons, bowls, masks, rattles, and even storage.

Go To These Exciting Indian Events in Our State

Circle of Nations Indian Association Annual Traditional Powwow – March, Morris; Annual Traditional Intertribal Bear Creek Pow – March, Rochester; Annual Cherish the Children – May, St Paul; White Earth Annual Pow-Wow – June, White Earth; Pipestone Dakota Community's Annual Tradition – July, Pipestone; Mille Lacs Band of Ojibwe Annual Pow Wow – August, Onamia; Annual Grand Portage Rendezvous Days – August, Grand Portage.

H is for . . .

Horn and Hooves

Indians used animal horn to make spoons and dishes. Hooves were made into rattles and bird beaks were used for decoration.

Hatchet

A small, short-handled ax, primarily used as a tool, not as a weapon. When settlers moved in, stone hatchets were replaced with iron ones.

Hair

Indians used hair as a textile. Hair from bison, mountain sheep, elk, moose, deer, dog, rabbit, beaver, or even humans were used to weave cloth, make wigs, or stuff pillows, balls, dolls or drumsticks.

Hole-in-the-Day

Famous Chippewa chief who fought the Dakota for the fishing and hunting grounds of Lake Superior. Finally drove the Dakota across the Mississippi River. Traveled to Washington, D.C. on many occasions for treaty negotiations. His band settled at the White Earth Reservation. Died in 1868.

Ho Chunk (Winnebago)

In 1993, the Ho-Chunk Nation reclaimed their original name which means "People of the Big Voice," or "People of the Sacred Language." "Winnebago" which means "People of the Stinky Waters" was a name given by the Sac (Sauk) and Fox people.

Hunters

Early Indian peoples were hunters who used wooden spears with stone points to kill many kinds of large mammals that are extinct today, such as mammoths and mastodons!

Horses

Spaniards brought the horse to America. At first, Indians were afraid of the horse or thought it was sacred. Later, Indians "broke" horses gently, often "hypnotizing" them with a blanket. Horses were used for transportation, trade, barter or payment. Some Indians ate horse meat in hopes of gaining the animal's power.

How it Happened

To record meetings and events, the Chippewa carved with a bone tool on bark scrolls, and used red paint for coloring.

Harvest

Minnesota Indians harvested wild rice by floating a canoe through the shallow water where rice grows. The Indian bent the grain heads over into the canoe and hit them with a stick to cause the grain to fall into the boat.

I is for . . .

Indian Wars

The U.S. War Department's list of official Indian wars includes the 1857 Sioux Indian disturbances in Minnesota and the 1862-7 Sioux War in Minnesota led by Chief Little Crow, which ended in the Indian's defeat and removal to a reservation.

Indian Mounds Park

In St. Paul; see well-preserved pyramid-shaped Indian mounds.

Indian Removal Act of 1830

This federal act gave President Andrew Jackson the power to relocate tribes east of the Mississippi to an "Indian Territory." The forced removal of the southeast Indians later became known as the "Trail of Tears."

Indian Treaties

After white settlers moved into Minnesota, the Dakota were forced to sign treaties at Traverse des Sioux and Pilot Knob. The treaty was signed in two locations to reduce the power of having all the chiefs at one location. A total of 35 chiefs signed over 24 million acres of land to the U.S. government. The Indians got two narrow reservations (150 miles long by 10 miles wide), later reduced by half, which led to great distrust of the whites by the Indians. During the Dakota Conflict of 1862, the U.S. government forced the Dakota out of the state. Some later returned to the Minnesota River Valley where their descendants live today.

Ioway

This tribe lived in Minnesota for a time. They were here in 1700, in the southwestern part of the state, near Red Pipestone Quarry. They moved frequently due to pressure from white settlers and other tribes.

Indian Ladder

Indians made ladders by trimming branches off a tree. Some were left at consistent intervals to provide steps.

Indian Tribes in Minnesota

At one time or another, these tribes have lived in the state of Minnesota:
Arapaho, Assiniboine, Cheyenne, Chippewa (Ojibway), Ioway, Omaha, Sioux, Winnebago

Indian

In 1493, Christopher Columbus called the native people he met in North America "Indians" because he mistakenly believed he had sailed to India! Today, this term includes the aborigines of North and South America.

J is for . . .

Just So You Know . . .

Today you can find many Minnesota Indians that follow some traditional ways. But there are also many who are entrepreneurs, doctors, lawyers, educators and even politicians! If you visit a reservation or cultural event, make sure you know visitor etiquette. Often dances are religious ceremonies and should be observed as such; religious dances should not be applauded. Photography, videotaping and drawing are all important issues - check with the tribe or individual before any is started.

Jesuits

Roman Catholic priests called Jesuits were among the first to meet and live with the North American Indians. Their writings, sent back to Europe, serve as one of today's best references to early Indian life.

Jeffers

Minnesota town and site of an ancient Indian civilization which carved around 2,000 pictures of animals, people and religious symbols on a local rocky ridge.

Judicial Termination

Modern term to describe current efforts by various U.S. government agencies and officials (especially the judicial system) to legally decrease the sovereignty of independent Indian tribes.

Just In Time!

The Indian Arts and Crafts Act of 1990 makes it against the law to pretend that an item has been made by Native Americans if it is really not. It is illegal to offer or display for sale, or sell any art or craft product in a way that falsely suggests it is Indian produced.

Jerked Meat

Thin strips of buffalo, elk, deer or other animal meat which is dried on racks in the sun; also called "jerky."

K is for . . .

Kill Site

An archaeological site where remains of many animals have been found along with human artifacts. Many kill sites have been useful to scientists in learning how ancient American Indians lived.

Kathio State Park

At Mille Lacs; site of the decisive Chippewa victory over the Dakota in a 1745 battle.

Killed Pottery

Pottery placed in a grave as an offering to the dead person was called killed pottery. A hole was formed in its base during creation. Often broken pottery was placed in a grave because Indians believed the spirit of the dead person would then be released and could travel.

Knife

Made from various materials such as bone, reed, stone, wood, antler, shell, metal, or animal teeth (bear, beaver, etc.), knives were used as weapons but also creative handiwork.

Koochiching County Historical Society Museum

International Falls; exhibits of prehistoric Indian artifacts.

Knots

Tied on bowstrings, spearhead and arrowhead lashings, snowshoes, and other items, knots were sometimes used to keep track of the days like a calendar—each knot equaled 1 day.

L is for . . .

Linguistic Families

There are 56 related groups of American Indian languages. A few of these speech families include Iroquoian, Algonquian, Siouan, Muskogean, Athapascan, and Wakashan.

Leggings

Both men and women wore cloth or skin covering, which were often decorated with quills, beads, or painted designs, for their legs.

Lost Tribes of Israel

This historic theory has been floating around since 721 BC. The 10 lost tribes of Israel are supposedly groups of people gathered together by Sargon, the King of Assyria. Some say he cast out 10 of the 12 tribes of Israel. Many have tried to prove that the American Indians are these missing tribes!

Lake Agassiz

A huge glacial lake that covered northern Minnesota thousands of years ago. The site where tiny bands of early peoples settled after a century-long migration by their ancestors from the Asia-North America land bridge.

Laurel Culture

The hunter-gatherers who lived west of International Falls at Grand Mound around 500 B.C. to A.D. 800. The Blackduck Culture may have evolved from this group.

Little Crow

Santee-Dakota Sioux chief and leader. He was also known as Taoyateduta, meaning "His People Are Red." He signed the treaty at Mendota, Minnesota in 1851, when the Dakota gave up most of their lands. As a Christian convert, Little Crow was a friend to settlers. But when promised food and supplies were delayed, the Dakota went on the warpath in 1862. Little Crow led them over 200 miles, killing many whites. He was finally defeated at Fort Ridgely and killed by a settler in 1863, near Hutchinson.

Land Loss

Native Americans lost their land in many ways. Conflicts with other tribes, colonization, European settlement, treaties, and removal took away Indian lands.

Lance

Spear used for hunting and war. The hunting lance had a short shaft and a broad, heavy head. The war lance was light and had a long shaft.

Lariat

These throw ropes made of rawhide, buffalo hair, or horsehair sometimes measured up to 20 feet long!

M is for . . .

Maize

Also called Indian Corn. Known as a "cereal" plant because it probably began as some form of grass. The Indians in our state figured out every possible way to use corn as a food. The only thing the white man added was the creation of "corn flakes!"

Maple Syrup

Harvested from the trees, the boiled sap we know as maple syrup was considered a delicacy among forest-dwelling Dakota Indians of early Minnesota.

Minnesota

The state and the river get their name from the Dakota word for "cloudy water" or "sky blue water."

Medicine

Medicine could be good or bad. Medicines or charms were placed in a bag by young warriors and carried at all times. Some of the roots, leaves and bark that Indians in our state used as medicine are being rediscovered and used by today's doctors!

Moccasins

Indian shoes made of animal skin.

Mille Lacs

North of today's town of Onamia. Former site of a large Dakota Indian settlement.

Mankato

Means "blue earth" in the Dakota language. Refers to the color of the veins of soil on the banks of the Blue Earth River. The Dakota Conflict ended in 1862 when Indians who had been convicted after the uprising were brought here to wait for a review of their cases by President Lincoln. He commuted 265 of the sentences; the other 38 Indians were hanged on December 26, the largest execution in the United States.

N is for . . .

Nomadic

A way of life in which people frequently moved from one location to another in search of food. "Seminomadic" people had permanent villages, but left them in certain seasons to hunt, fish, or gather wild plant foods.

Needle

The kind of needle we think of for sewing was very rare among the Indians. They did have some needles made from bone, wood, cactus spines and the locust tree. The iron needle was brought over with the settlers. Thread used included horsehair, human hair and plant fibers.

Nation

There are many Indian nations located within the United States, such as the Red Lake Nation. Indian nations are called nations because their governments and laws are independent of and separate from the U.S. government. The federal government must have "government to government" relations with these Indian nations, just as it would with foreign nations, like England or Spain.

November

In 1990, President George Bush approved a joint resolution designating November 1990 "National American Indian Heritage Month." Similar proclamations have been issued each year since 1994.

Names

Indian names were often changed during one's lifetime. These names could be derived from events that happened during the person's birth, childhood, adolescence, war service, or retirement from active tribal life. Some names came from dreams, some were inherited, and sometimes names were stolen or taken in revenge. Today some Indians maintain old, traditional Indian names, while others take modern names. Since settlers often did not read or write Indian languages, they recorded Indian names phonetically (as they "sounded"). Thus Indian names were often misspelled.

National Museum of the American Indian

The Smithsonian's National Museum of the American Indian on the National Mall in Washington, D.C., symbolizes a deeper understanding between America's first citizens and those who have come to make these shores their home.

New Ulm

Site of an 1862 Dakota Conflict when more than 1,000 settlers poured in as a group of volunteers was setting up makeshift fortifications. The citizen soldiers were able to hold off about 100 Dakota on August 19 and 650 on August 23, but 30 of the soldiers were killed and 60 injured.

O is for . . .

Ojibway

Also spelled Ojibwa or Ojibwe; this is the Canadian name for the Chippewa. In the late 1600s, they began pushing their way into the state from the St. Lawrence River. Driven west by tribal warfare from the European fur trade. These Indians were traders, trappers and excellent canoeists.

Old Bones

No one knows for sure when the first people came to North America, but scientists have dated bones and artifacts discovered at Clovis, New Mexico around 11,200 years old. Testing on a skeleton found on the Channel Islands, off the coast of California showed they were about 13,000 years old. And, evidence of human habitation in southern New Mexico suggests that people may have been there as far back as 38,000 years ago.

Oil

Indians extracted oil from the many layers of fat that came with fresh bear meat. The fat was boiled down in earthen pots to produce the oil, which was stored in gourds and pots. The oil was used for cooking and even beautifying the body! Indians would mix red pigment with the oil, add the fragrances of cinnamon and sassafras, and rub it all over their bodies.

Origins

Some scientists believe that Native Americans actually came across a land bridge between Asia and North America. They say that during an ice age thousands of years ago, the water level was much lower and people could have walked between the two continents.

Omaha

This was another tribe that lived for a while close to the Pipestone Quarry in southern Minnesota. Primarily villagers and farmers, but they also fished and hunted. The Omaha were also known for having many rules about social behavior.

Orators

Many Indian leaders were excellent public speakers. Powerful and dramatic speakers were vital to leaders who wanted to influence their tribe. Watch for famous Indian quotations in literature and textbooks!

Office of Indian Education Programs

This is a service organization devoted to providing quality education opportunities for American Indian people. Established in the latter part of the nineteenth century to carry out the federal government's education commitment to Indian tribes, it has become the only national education system for American Indian children and adults.

P is for . . .

Powwow

The original form of the word meant "medicine man." Medicine men would often use noise motion and confusion to scare away harmful spirits and cure people. It was also a gathering to talk about political matters. Today, the powwow is an event where Indians gather to sing, perform ceremonial dances, and share cultural pride and traditions.

Pipestone National Monument

For centuries, Indians of the Great Lakes and Mississippi and Missouri valleys traveled to this quarry to get red stone for carving calumets.

Prairie du Chein

Wisconsin; site an 1825 treaty setting boundaries between Chippewa and Sioux lands in Minnesota. Made it easier to take away lands later. The Arrowhead Chippewa lost their land in 1837 and 1854 treaties. More was lost in 1866 after iron was discovered on the Vermilion Reservation. The Chippewa in northwestern Minnesota sold their lands in the Red River Valley in 1863.

Paint

Indians used many natural materials to make paint, like clay mixed with oil or grease. Yellow "paint" was made with the gall bladder of a buffalo! Why did they paint their faces or bodies? Indians used paint to look scary or beautiful, to disguise themselves, or to protect their skin from sunburn or insect bites. Indians often applied red paint because it symbolized strength and success.

Pipestone County Historical Museum

Here you can see Indian ceremonial pipes, headdresses and beaded and quilled clothing from the Dakota and Ojibwa tribes.

Pemmican

Indian food made of animal meat, which was dried in the sun, pounded together with fat and berries. The mixture was packed into skin bags and used primarily while on the trail.

Papoose

An American Indian infant aged between birth and one year is called a papoose. A papoose spent most of his or her days snugly wrapped in a kind of cradle made of skins or bark and a wooden frame that hung on the mother's back. This sturdy frame also allowed a mother to lean her papoose against a tree or rock within sight as she worked.

Picture History

Some Indians kept a record of time and important events by painting or drawing pictures or symbols on skin, bark, or stone.

Pottery

Indian pottery was made from built-up spirals of clay that were molded or paddled, or a combination of the two methods. Most pottery served as cooking vessels.

Q is for . . .

Quillwork

Indians used the quills of porcupine or birds to make a type of embroidery. Quills were dyed with juice from berries and other materials. When they were ready to be used, the quills were either mashed with teeth or softened with hot water and flattened with rocks. The quills were then laced into moccasins, shirts, pipe covers, and other items. Beads which Indians received by trading with settlers eventually replaced quillwork.

Quality

Native American arts and crafts are known for their excellent craftsmanship and striking designs. This work is often influenced by things found in nature especially plants and animals.

Quotations

"Come, it is time for you to depart. We are going on a long journey." — Death song sung by Chippewa warriors in old Minnesota

"If they are hungry, let them eat grass." — Unsympathetic comment by an Indian agent's trader to the Dakota at the Lower Sioux Agency who found themselves starving when the agent refused to hand out the government's food for the Indians in 1862.

Quiver

Case used to hold arrows; made of woven plant materials or animal skins.

Quirt

A short riding whip with a wood, bone, or horn handle.

R is for . . .

Rain Dancing

The rain dance ceremony, performed to encourage rainfall, was common among Indian religions because good weather is vital for a successful harvest. Rainmakers were in tune with nature; there are actual reported cases of Indians producing or preventing rain!

Roots

Indians used plant roots for food, medicine, dye, baskets, cloth, rope, salt, flavoring, and just to chew!

Rattles

Indians of Minnesota made rattles from bird beaks, animal hooves, bones, pods, seashells, turtle shells and other animal parts. The rattles are used in ceremonies.

Rivalry

The Chippewa and the Sioux waged war off and on for almost 100 years, with tragic consequences for both. By 1750, the Chippewa controlled the northern part of Minnesota, having pushed the Sioux to the southwest part of the region.

Rawhide

Untanned animal hide. The "green" hide was stretched on the ground or over a frame. Flesh and fat were removed. The skin was dried, washed, then buried with wood ashes which made the hair come off. Used by the Minnesota Indian to make drumheads, lash lodge poles, mend broken objects and in many other ways.

Reservations

The U.S. government set aside, or "reserved," land for the Indians. These reservations originally served as a sort of prison during the beginning stages of Indian removal. At that time, reservations provided the government with some control over Indian activity and residency. This land was usually considerably less desirable land than the Indians' native territories. Today's reservations are lands that are tribally held, yet protected by the government.

Red Wing

Named for a Dakota chief whose name meant "wild swan's wing dyed scarlet."

S is for . . .

Sign Language
A way for Indians to communicate with others from a tribe whose language they did not speak.

Shaman
Medicine man and spiritual leader who was supposed to have special healing power from another world.

Secret Societies
Indians had secret groups, usually organized for religious or ceremonial reasons. Each society had a purpose, such as to cure disease.

Sweatlodge
Structure used for ritual purification by sweating from exposure to very hot fires or hot steam from pouring water over hot stones. Also called a sweathouse, for some tribes also doubling as clubhouses.

Shield
A piece of "armor" made of a rawhide-covered frame, which was carried into battle. Shields also could be decorative and religious objects. Many tribes make shields today as an art form!

Stone-boiling
Cooking method by placing preheated stones into cooking vessels.

Sacred Bundles
A group of objects treasured by a tribe. They were well-guarded and often taken into battle. The items were publicly shown only on very important occasions.

Saddle
While some Indians did use saddles on their horses, most rode bareback!

Signals
Indian signs made with a pony, blanket, mirror, smoke, fire-arrow or other item to communicate over long distances.

Sioux
This tribe is made up of different groups with varying histories and customs. They were driven west by the Chippewa, from the upper Mississippi River area. The Sioux are collectively known as the Dakota. There are four ancestral branches of the Sioux, each containing different bands. The tribe is the most famous of the Plains warriors, and it is their image we see so often in art and films. The group living in Minnesota are sometimes called the Eastern Sioux.

Santee Sioux
Another name for the Dakota Indians of Minnesota.

T is for . . .

Tobacco

A sacred plant early Indians used to make offering to their gods, cure diseases, bring good luck, seal agreements and bind treaties.

Treaties

Written agreements between the U. S. government and the Indians, most of which involved the Indians giving up their native lands.

Throwing Stick

A sling or grooved stick used to hurl a lance or spear. It was used by Minnesota Indians before bows and arrows.

Totem

The spirit of some natural object (usually an animal) taken by an Indian, tribe or family to guard over them.

Tomahawk

A club, axe or hammer used to chop wood, drive stakes in the ground or as a weapon.

Tepees

Minnesota's Dakota Indians built skin-covered homes which were east to set up and take down as they changed locations from season to season.

Tracking

To follow a trail by finding a sign such as a broken blade of grass, a moved stone or moccasin track. Indians learned to trail as children, so that they could find food, track enemies and disguise their own signs.

Teeth

Minnesota Indians hung teeth on cords to make necklaces.

Tribal Entity

An example is the Minnesota Chippewa Tribe which is composed of 6 separate bands of Indians, with each band being considered an individual entity for some purposes.

Tribe

A group of Indians with shared culture, history, original territory, ancestry, social organization, and governmental structure. A tribe may contain several bands of Indians.

Thunderbird

A mythological Indian figure, as well as a part of the constellations for many Indians. Thunderbird mythology is mostly different from tribe to tribe, in general either coexisting with ancestors as an actual bird, or appearing as a spiritual nature god. The Thunderbird was good to the people in either case. Much mythology ties the thunderbird with thunder, lightning and storms.

U is for . . .

U.S. Bureau of Indian Affairs

Provides public services such as law enforcement, land records, economic development, and education to Indians. Known for mismanagement and ethical problems.

U.S. Army

Many Native Americans have fought bravely for the United States Army. Many have also given their lives for a country that was not always accepting of them.

U.S. Coins

The profile of a Sioux Indian, in full eagle headdress and fringed shirt, is featured on the 1859-1909 U.S. penny and the 1916-1938 U.S. nickel.

U.S. Indian Schools

The Bureau of Indian Affairs operates hundreds of federal schools around the nation. Enrollment of Native American children measures in the thousands!

U.S. Indian Reorganization Act

Passed by Congress in 1934, the act authorized Indian tribes to establish and conduct their own governments, and to form businesses.

Upper and Lower Sioux Agencies

Established in the Minnesota Valley in 1853 to change the Dakota Indians from a nomadic lifestyle to a farming lifestyle. After a poor crop in 1861, the Indians nearly starved the next year, getting no sympathy from the whites, and confrontations started.

U.S. President

Once called Great White Father by Indians.

U.S. Indian Wars

The U.S. War Department has compiled an official list of "Indian Wars" that occurred in the United States. Over 50 wars were fought between the U.S. and the Indians during the period of 1790-1850.

V is for . . .

Vessels

Indians carried water in special gourds shaped liked bottles, called water vessels.

Village Councils

These were held in the town (council) house and occurred to discuss and decide important matters. Harmony and agreement was essential to tribal unity. Rather than vote on issues, they were discussed until everyone was satisfied. Anyone who wanted to could speak freely. Everyone did not always agree on the outcome, but everyone avoided conflict by pushing their case.

Vegetable Dyes

Indians could not buy color from the store like we can today. Instead, they created many different colors from the things they found on earth like plants, flowers, shrubs, trees, roots, and berries. They made beautiful and unique reds, oranges, yellows, greens, browns, and violets. These dyes were used for baskets, pottery, weaving, body makeup, and clothing.

Vineland

Site of the Mille Lacs Indian Museum; exhibits, dioramas and displays of Chippewa crafts.

Villages

Many Minnesota Indians lived in villages! Villages were formed around different clans or bands within the tribe, but could also contain different clans living together. Villages were usually permanent settlements, although semi-nomadic tribes have been known to migrate between permanent villages. Dakota Indians often lived on the grasslands in summer and moved to the forests in winter.

Vesperic Indians

Indian tribes located in the United States.

W is for . . .

War Bonnet

Special headdress worn into battle, often adorned with feathers.

War Pony

Horse, often painted with colorful paint and ridden into battle.

Wood Lake Battle

September 23, 1862 on the Minnesota River; 1,600 infantry and volunteers forced Dakota Indians protesting starvation to retreat.

War Dance

Indian braves danced this before going into battle. The dance was a way of assembling the braves and getting them to commit to the fight ahead.

Winnebago

This central Great Lakes woodland tribe lived in villages of rectangular bark lodges, but also went on the trail to hunt buffalo. They hunted, fished, gathered and farmed for their food. The "Winnebago Way" means to live with a reverence for nature. After the Black Hawk war many were relocated—some to Minnesota.

Woodland Era

Around 500 B.C.; period of time when the mound-building civilization spread into Minnesota. There were once more than 10,000 mounds in our state. Many vanished beneath the plows of farmers or vandalism, but some also remain today.

Whistle

Indians from Minnesota made them from the wing bones of birds. The whistles made the sound of the bird the bones came from! Used to communicate, signal, sound an alarm or even flirt with a maiden!

War Club

A weapon made of stone, bone, or wood in the shape of a club.

White Man

Indians generally called them Pale Face, a name the white men themselves suggested!

Wild Rice

A major food source for the Sioux, Chippewa, and other Great Lakes Indians. They began to harvest wild rice on shallow lakes and marshes around A.D. 500.

XYZ are for . . .

Xenophobe

A xenophobe is someone who is afraid of foreign people, their customs and cultures, or foreign things. Many of the first European settlers were afraid of Native American cultures.

You Bet!

Some Native Americans say that Casinos make a lot of money. Others say that too many people have a gambling problem. In the 1980s and 1990s, many tribes discussed whether or not gambling casinos should be allowed. Now that many casinos have been built across the country, the debate has switched to how it should be controlled.

Zounds!

Between 1871 and 1913, at least 98 traditional agreements between tribes and the United States were negotiated and 96 of them were ratified by Congress. Each agreement remains as law (unless changed by a later agreement)!

ZZZZZZ...

Shamans and medicine men were not the only people who had access to the spirit world. Indians believed that people could make contact with spirits every night in their dreams! Dreamers could travel back to the time of man's creation or far ahead into their own futures. They also believed that dreams contained warnings or commands from the spirits. Many tribes felt that they had to act out their dreams as soon as they awoke. If an Indian dreamed about bathing, for example, he would run to his neighbors' houses first thing in the morning, and his neighbors would throw kettles full of cold water over him.

Y... Or, "Why?"

1. Why do you think Indian warriors carried charms with them? Some Indian medicines have been scientifically proven to have true healing power and are still used today. Do you think their charms had any real power to help them win battles?
2. Why do you think the American government kept relocating Indians onto reservations and then making the reservations smaller and smaller?
3. Why did Indians use items such as a pipe in ceremonies? What kinds of symbolic objects do we use in ceremonies today?
4. Why and how did Indians use natural materials in creative ways?
5. Many Indian tribes are running successful businesses on their reservations today. There is one industry that many tribes are making a lot of money at. Do you know what this is? Hint: "I'll bet you do!"

Which Famous Native American Am I?

Solve the puzzle!

Word Bank

Black Elk	Crazy Horse	Sitting Bull	Sequoia
Sacajawea	Chief Joseph	Geronimo	Pocahontas

Down

1. This Shoshone woman joined Lewis and Clark as their guide and translator and helped make the expedition a success! Hint: She has 4 "a"s in her name!
4. This man gave the Cherokee their first alphabet so that they could write. Until then, they communicated only by speaking and drawing pictures. Hint: A famous ancient tree also has the same name!
5. He was one of the fiercest of Indian warriors! He fought against white settlers in Arizona and New Mexico to keep his people from being pushed off their lands. Hint: Jump!

Across

2. A legend says that this brave Algonquian woman saved the life of Englishman John Smith. Hint: Disney produced a movie about her.
3. He fought at Little Bighorn when he was only 13! He was also a wise "shaman" who saw visions and could advise people. Hint: Part of his name is an animal with antlers!
6. He was a great Sioux warrior who won the battle against General Custer at Little Bighorn in 1876. Hint: His horse was not crazy!
7. A leader of the Lakota (Sioux) tribe who lived on the Standing Rock Reservation in North Dakota after the battle of Little Bighorn. He tried to make conditions better for his people there, so the U.S. government called him a "troublemaker." Hint: He did not sit all the time!
8. A wise and brave chief of the Nez Percé who tried to bring his people to Canada to escape war. He said, "From where the sun now stands, I will fight no more forever." Hint: His father's name was "Old Joseph."

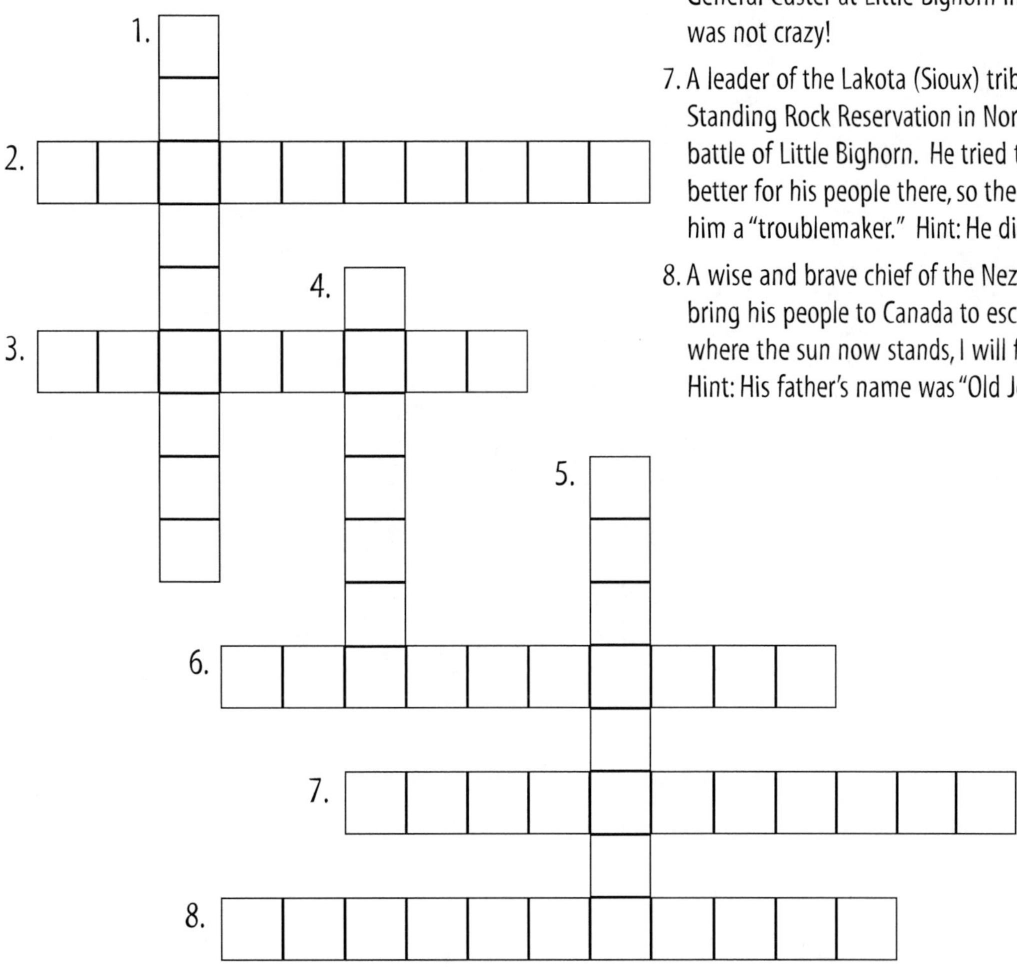

Answer Key: 1. Sacajawea; 2. Pocahontas; 3. Black Elk; 4. Sequoia; 5. Geronimo; 6. Crazy Horse; 7. Sitting Bull; 8. Chief Joseph

Different Ways for Different Indians!

North American Indian tribes are divided into different areas. In each of these areas, tribes shared common ways of living with each other. They might make similar arts or crafts, they might eat the same foods, or they might have had the same beliefs. These activities are all part of their "culture." Each area had its own culture, which was different from the tribes in all the other areas.

Below is a map of all the different groups of Indian tribes in North America. Color each area with a different color. You will see a colorful picture of how Native Americans can all be called "Indians" but still have very different cultures!

Celebration!

Powwows are big festivals where Native Americans gather to sing, dance, and eat together. It is a time to celebrate and show pride in their culture. Powwows can last from one afternoon to several days. The Indians dress in native costumes and dance ancient dances to the beating of drums.

Artists sell their arts and crafts. You might be able to buy some real Native American food cooked on an open fire. Native Americans go to powwows to be with each other, share ideas, and just have fun! Most powwows are also open to people who are not Indian. It's a great place to learn about Native American culture!

If you went to a powwow this weekend, what do you think you would see? What do you think might NOT be there? Circle the objects you think you would see at a powwow. Put an X through those you probably won't see.

Answer Key: Circled objects are: beads, moccasins, open fire, drums, feathers, baskets, kids, food, drums, horse.

Make an Indian Weaving!

Many Native Americans used weaving to create useful things like sashes (belts), bags, mats, and blankets. They used animal hair to make yarn, and dyed the yarn with natural dyes from fruits and other plants. They also used some plant fibers, like cotton, to make weaving thread.

Weave a small Native American mat of your own. Use different colors of yarn to create a beautiful pattern in your weaving. Place a favorite object on the mat or hang it on your wall!

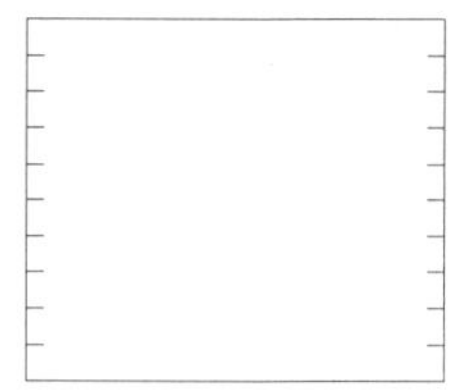

Prepare the "loom"

Cut a piece of cardboard 5 inches wide and 6 inches long. Along the two 5-inch sides (the "short" sides), have an adult cut slits 1/4 inch deep. These slits should be 1/2 inch apart from each other. So, on each short side you will have 9 slits.

Directions:

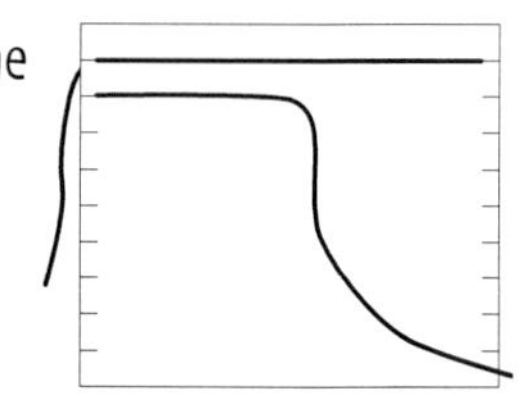

1. Take a long piece of yarn and bring it from the back through the first slit (the one next to the edge of the cardboard.) The end of the yarn will hang down behind the cardboard.

2. Bring the yarn right across the front of the cardboard to the slit opposite the one your yarn came through.

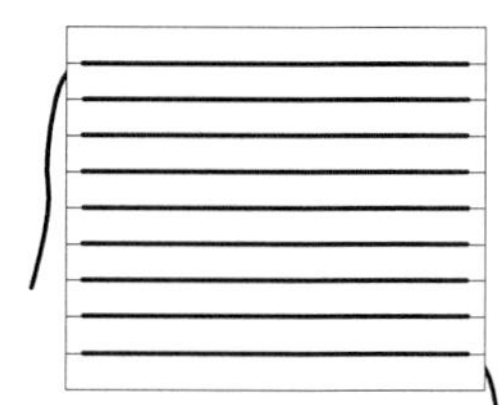

3. Now bring the yarn under the back of the cardboard and then up again through the second slit.

4. Repeat #2 and #3, until you have 9 strands of yarn across the front of your cardboard!

5. Then cut the yarn and tie the two loose ends in the back of the cardboard.

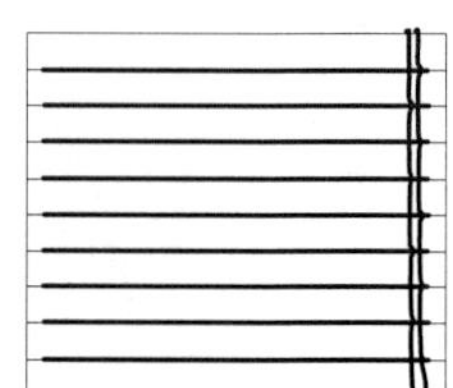

6. Take another piece of yarn and start feeding it through the 9 strands, going over one, under the next over the next, etc. When you get to the end, pull the yarn behind the cardboard and around to the front, and begin again. This time, whatever strand you went over, go under. And whatever strand you went under, go over.

7. Repeat this pattern until the front of your cardboard in covered. Then cut the yarn in the back of the cardboard, and trim it to create a fringe for your mat!

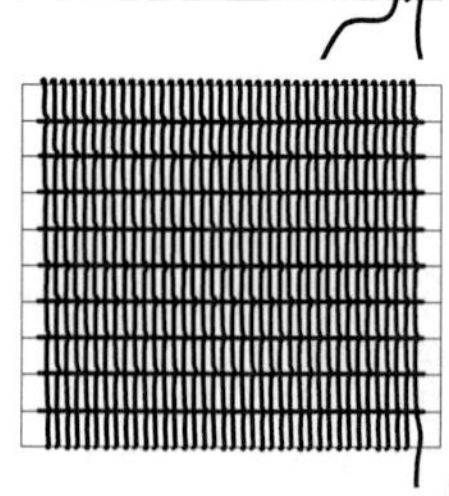

Tips:

- For a wild look, use variegated or different colored yarn!
- For a tighter mat, push the under/over strands up against the previous strands during weaving.
- To keep your mat from unravelling, tie neighboring fringe together up close to the mat.

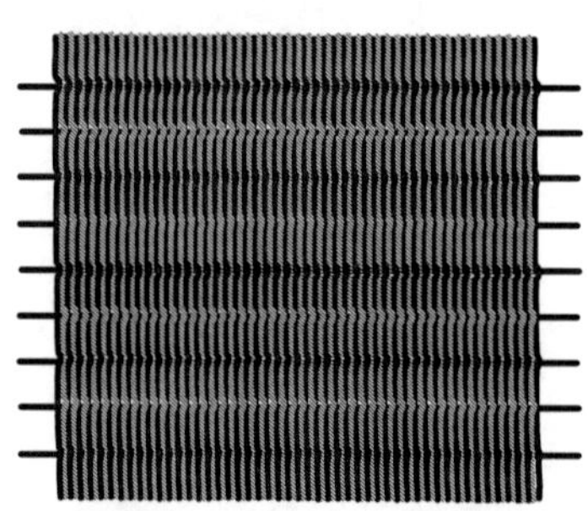

Finders Keepers?

Native Americans have many buried treasures. For hundreds of years, special objects would sometimes be buried with Native Americans, or maybe they would just be lost. Archeologists used to dig for interesting artifacts in old Native American gravesites. They would keep the Native American bones or the arrowheads, rattles, masks and other objects that they found. But this made the Native Americans feel like they were being robbed.

In 1990, the U.S. government passed a law that said that no one could look for or take these Native American objects anymore. And whoever had any already had to give them back to the people they belonged to. This is called repatriation

Help the archeologist return the artifact to a Native American.

Fast Fact

An artifact is an object that was made by people a long time ago for some useful purpose.

Busy Hands!

Before modern times, Native Americans didn't have stores where they went to buy things. They made everything they needed.

What did Indians make with their own hands? Use the Word Bank and pictures to find out!

Word Bank

blanket	moccasins	arrows	pottery	canoe
mat	food	jewelry	pouch	box

 ___ ___ ___

 ___ ___ ___ ___

 ___ ___ ___

 ___ ___ ___ ___ ___

 ___ ___ ___ ___ ___ ___ ___

 ___ ___ ___ ___ ___

 ___ ___ ___ ___ ___ ___ ___ ___ ___ ___

 ___ ___ ___ ___ ___ ___

 ___ ___ ___ ___ ___ ___ ___

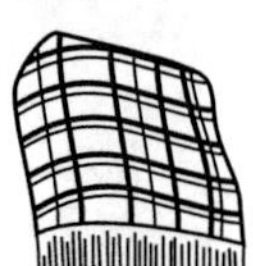 ___ ___ ___ ___ ___ ___ ___

American Indians Today

Beginning with the first letter of each group of letters, cross out every other letter to discover some new words. You may not have heard of these before, but you can read all about them!

1. Many Indians live on these, but many more do not!

TRYELSDEBRNVJAOTPIPOWNASX

____

2. Many Indians have been poor for a long time because for many years the government took away their lands and their ability to make a living.

TPKOOVWEBRNTXYA

____

3. Many Indians have been studying hard at school and going to college in order to earn more money. Education helps the Indians make their lives better. These Native Americans are working to become:

TSJUMCBCFEYSMSOFPUVL

____

4. This is a big term that means Native Americans have worked hard to get the U.S. government to let them rule themselves. This means that they have their own laws and make their own decisions. They are like a separate country inside the U.S.! Now, try and see if you can get your parents to give you the same thing!

TSGENLBF **JDGEETSEWRAMCIHNUAKTYIKOTNU**

______________ ______________________________

Fast Fact

What do Indians work as today?

- doctors
- nurses
- factory workers
- artists
- lawyers
- actors

The same kinds of jobs any American might work at!

Native Americans Move to the City!

Solve the code to discover the mystery words!

A	B	C	D	E	F	G	H	I	J	K	L	M
✷	❀	⌘	♣	➽	♥	❗	✯	✂	✆	☛	✈	✉
N	**O**	**P**	**Q**	**R**	**S**	**T**	**U**	**V**	**W**	**X**	**Y**	**Z**
✿	✩	◆	✡	✏	❦	☎	✒	✚	✖	✍	✠	✓

1. During the 1950s and 1960s, the American government paid Indians to leave their homes on reservations and move to cities to get jobs. If cities are sometimes called urban areas, then these brave Indians were called:

___ ___ ___ ___ ___   ___ ___ ___ ___ ___ ___ ___

✒ ✏ ❀ ✷ ✿   ✂ ✿ ♣ ✂ ✷ ✿ ❦

2. Many Indians chose to stay on their reservations and not move to the city. They thought that if they moved to the city, they would lose the way of life that their parents and ancestors had taught. These Indians called themselves:

___ ___ ___ ___ ___ ___ ___ ___ ___ ___ ___   ___ ___ ___ ___ ___ ___ ___

✏ ➽ ❦ ➽ ✏ ✚ ✷ ☎ ✂ ✩ ✿   ✂ ✿ ♣ ✂ ✷ ✿ ❦

3. Native Americans who moved to cities lived close to each other. They tried to keep their way of life as much as possible. They did not want to forget their religion, native art, or music. They did not want to lose their:

___ ___ ___ ___ ___ ___ ___

⌘ ✒ ✈ ☎ ✒ ✏ ➽

4. Are you afraid of heights? Many people are. The Mohawk Indians are not! Many of them work hundreds of feet above the city to build steel frames for skyscrapers. People who do this work above the city are:

___ ___ ___ ___ ___   ___ ___ ___ ___ ___ ___ ___

❦ ☎ ➽ ➽ ✈   ✖ ✩ ✏ ☛ ➽ ✏ ❦

5. Today urban Indians and reservation Indians come together to celebrate their culture. They share ideas and stories. They dance and beat drums. They make and sell Indian jewelry. During these celebrations, Indians remember how much they have to be proud of! These big parties are called

___ ___ ___ ___ ___ ___ ___

◆ ✩ ✖ ✖ ✩ ✖ ❦